the boy who burned too brightly

A Modern Allegory

WRITTEN BY DR. DAVID J. WELSH

— ◆ —

ILLUSTRATED BY BRANDON BOLT

Alisam Press ◆ Fort Worth, Texas

Published by:
Alisam Press
6040 Camp Bowie, Suite 52
Fort Worth, TX 76116
(817) 735-8299

Printed in the United States of America
March, 1997 first printing
March, 2001 second printing

Library of Congress Catalog Card Number 97-92930
ISBN 0-9656442-0-0

Book design by Tim Bolt

To my wife Beverly,

whose unwavering confidence and support

have kept my flame burning brightly for 25 years.

When he was born, Randall's parents thought he was perfect in every way. Of course he had the customary number of fingers, toes, eyes, hands, and all the other appropriate body parts. And, like everyone in Flintville, Randall also had a flame burning on top of his head. However, Randall's flame glimmered and shimmered with a particularly warm and friendly glow. The McBlythes agreed it was the most extraordinary flame they had ever seen.

Randall grew into a happy and healthy boy. He enjoyed life and in turn was enjoyed by others. He developed a quick wit and an active imagination. And when Randall was excited or amused or curious, his flame would burn very brightly. At bedtime, Randall's parents often wished his flame would burn less brightly. If he had chores, Randall's flame might disappear altogether! But his parents loved the unpredictability of Randall's flame, and how it expressed his mood and personality.

As he grew older, Randall learned to make interesting designs with his flame. Simple shapes like squares, circles — even hearts — were no problem at all. But Randall could also create spectacular effects like fountains and fireworks. He could even juggle three

small fireballs at one time! With each new design or effect, Randall's parents laughed and applauded. They took great pride in their son's creativity and enjoyed watching others react to Randall's antics.

4

Unfortunately, there were times when Randall's flame bothered the adults around him. In church, for example, Randall's designs and tricks were definitely not appreciated. "Your son's flame is bothering us," the grownups often complained to Randall's parents. Then the McBlythes would ask Randall to dim his flame. And he would — for a few minutes. But soon he grew bored and would begin experimenting with new designs. And the people around him whispered and glared.

On Randall's first day of school, his parents were bursting with pride.

He looked like such a big boy in his new school clothes, and his eyes

sparkled with anticipation. From the way his flame danced and

fluttered, they could tell Randall was excited about his new adventure.

The McBlythes were especially happy that his teacher would be Mrs.

Steadfast, respected by all the parents of Flintville as a kind and loving

educator with many years of experience.

As the weeks went by, Randall's appetite for learning grew. Each time he told his mother about the interesting things that happened at school that day, his flame nearly crackled with energy. But on Fridays, Randall's weekly progress reports contained check marks for *burns too brightly, burns inconsistently,* and *inappropriate designs.* When his parents discussed these marks with Randall, his eyes watered and he promised to do better.

One day Mrs. Steadfast requested a conference to discuss Randall's progress. When they arrived, the McBlythes were surprised by what they heard. "Randall is a sweet boy who really is trying his best," Mrs. Steadfast began. "But he has problems with overall flame quality. Sometimes his flame burns so much brighter than the other children's. And he makes highly unusual designs. So he distracts the other children and doesn't keep his mind on his work. If I stand right by him and remind him to control his flame, then he improves somewhat. But I can't devote all my attention to Randall with twenty other students in the room! I'm quite worried about him."

The McBlythes did not know what to say. They were alarmed, but also puzzled. "Is Randall having trouble learning?" his mother asked. "Not exactly," Mrs. Steadfast replied. "It's just that he could be doing so much better if his flame burned less brightly and more consistently. Eventually his self-esteem may begin to suffer. To tell you the truth," she went on, "I think he may have Defective Flicker Syndrome — what's known as DFS. I have several students in the room with DFS, and the poor things all seem to have some sort of problem maintaining appropriate flames."

The McBlythes had never heard of DFS before. In fact, they had never thought Randall had any sort of problem. But Mrs. Steadfast was clearly concerned and very experienced, so they asked for more information. "Of course I'm not a doctor," she said, "so you would want a medical opinion. But I do have pamphlets and brochures you can read for more information. And we have a very active DFS support group meeting every week in the library." She gave the reading material to the McBlythes and told them the next meeting date of the support group. She thanked them for their commitment to helping Randall reach his true potential.

That night the McBlythes discussed Mrs. Steadfast's concerns. "What if he does have a problem which could be treated?" his mother asked. "I was just like him at that age," his father replied. "He'll grow out of it." "This brochure says DFS may be genetic," Randall's mother pointed out, "but with proper treatment the symptoms can be managed." Mr. McBlythe reached for the remote control. "And what is the treatment?" he asked. "A chemical additive called quiescence helps the flame burn more consistently and less brightly." "I think we're overreacting," yawned Mr. McBlythe. "But if it will make you feel better, call Dr. Kindle in the morning."

Dr. Kindle's waiting room was crowded when Randall and his mother arrived. He welcomed them into the examination room with a warm smile, and asked how Randall was feeling. "Oh I feel just fine," Randall replied, "Watch this!" And with that his flame emitted a bright shower of sparks into the air. Dr. Kindle chuckled. "You certainly have an amazing flame Randall." He winked and whispered, "Careful you don't burn the office down." Then he turned to Mrs. McBlythe. "And how are things at school?" he asked. "Well that's really why we're here today," she replied as she lowered her voice. "His teacher has noticed some irregularities in Randall's flame."

"What sort of irregularities?" asked Dr. Kindle. "Mrs. Steadfast says that Randall's flame burns too brightly and inconsistently. When he makes designs with his flame he's not doing his work." Dr. Kindle grew thoughtful. "Sounds like possible Defective Flicker Syndrome." Mrs. McBlythe flinched. "How do we know for sure?" she asked. Dr. Kindle pulled a paper from his drawer. "Answer these questions. This will tell us if he has DFS. If he does, we can begin treatment... and the sooner, the better." On the way home Randall asked, "Mommy, what's wrong with me?" She patted his hand and smiled reassuringly. "I don't know, sweetheart. But we're going to find out... and fix it."

That night Randall's mother attended a meeting of the DFS support group. She was surprised at the number of people, including Mrs. Steadfast and the school counselor. She also recognized the mothers of other boys in Randall's classroom. Before the meeting began, she browsed through the many books and tapes on the display table at the back of the room.

23

The meeting was called to order and the guest speaker was introduced. She was a local pyrologist and well-known specialist in Defective Flicker Syndrome — Dr. Vaticinate. Her appearance was sponsored by the local distributor of quiescence. Dr. Vaticinate spoke at length about the often-subtle symptoms of DFS. She explained that the disorder could be diagnosed easily by an expert asking the right questions. She reassured the audience that appropriate treatment quickly produced normal levels of functioning. After her speech, Dr. Vaticinate passed out business cards. Everyone was impressed with her obvious knowledge and experience.

When his mother came home that night, Randall greeted her at the door in his pajamas. "Hi, Mom! I waited up to show you a new trick. Watch this!" And Randall's flame began to burn with a rainbow of brilliant colors. But instead of the usual smile of delight, this time a worried look appeared on Mrs. McBlythe's face. "That's nice dear," she said weakly. But as she watched him scamper upstairs to bed, she worried. "Maybe he does burn a little too brightly." She pulled out the questions Dr. Kindle had given her. Then she picked up the telephone and dialed the number on Dr. Vaticinate's card.

"Where are we going?" Randall asked his mother the next morning as they got into the car. "We're going to see a special doctor, Randall." "But why? Am I sick?" "No," replied his mother, "she's not that kind of doctor. She's a pyrologist. She knows all about children's flames, and she can help us decide what to do about yours." "OK," shrugged Randall, who spent the rest of the drive practicing a new spiral design.

When they arrived, Dr. Vaticinate told Randall to wait in her playroom while she visited with his mother. When Randall saw all the toys, his flame sparkled and danced. As soon as they were seated, Dr. Vaticinate asked, "Does his flame always burn so brightly?" "Often it does," replied Mrs. McBlythe, "and his teacher has noticed the same thing." "I'm not surprised," replied Dr. Vaticinate. "A flame burning that brightly would surely cause problems in a classroom." She pulled out a paper and said, "Let's work on this questionnaire." "I've already done that," said Mrs. McBlythe as she pulled the same piece of paper from her purse.

"Well then, let's take a look." As Dr. Vaticinate read Mrs. McBlythe's responses, she nodded her head. "Just as I thought. Your son has a classic case of DFS." "How can you tell for sure?" asked Randall's mother. "Your responses," replied the respected pyrologist. "For example, you've indicated here that Randall's flame often contains unusual designs and colors... often burns brightly enough to bother other people... does not burn consistently. These observations are consistent with a diagnosis of DFS." Then she leaned forward with a knowing smile. "But frankly, I could have told you that simply by looking at the child."

"So what should we do?" asked Randall's mother. Dr. Vaticinate began typing on her computer keyboard. As she hit the 'print' button she said, "I will send Dr. Kindle my written report. You should call him and ask about starting Randall on quiescence. Within a very short period of time, his flame quality should improve and he will be able to succeed in school." "But how do I explain this to Randall?" asked his mother. "Just tell him he will be drinking something special to help him control his flame better and be more like the other children in his class. Tell him he's not a bad boy — he's just a boy who needs some extra help."

And so Randall began drinking a glass of quiescence every morning before he left the house, and another glass at school before lunch. Dr. Kindle was glad to write the prescription, noting that "it's quite harmless...and if it helps Randall get along better at school, it will certainly be worthwhile." Randall's father was skeptical, but willing to try the experiment. As for Mrs. Steadfast, she was delighted! In fact, she sent home a note saying that "Randall's flame is now burning much less brightly and much more consistently. Let's keep up the good work!"

One morning Mrs. McBlythe (an active school volunteer)

shared playground duty with Mrs. Turbeaux, whose son

Tony was one of Randall's classmates. As they watched the

children play, Mrs. McBlythe noticed that Tony seemed to

be having some problems. In fact, he was running from

one side of the playground to another, frantically chasing his own flame! As soon as he caught the flame and placed it back on his head, it would immediately jump off and lead him on yet another frustrating chase. Tony panted and sweated as he pursued his flame around the playground.

"Oh dear," said Tony's mother. "I knew I forgot something." "What's the problem?" asked Mrs. McBlythe. "I forgot to give Tony his special drink this morning, and now the poor thing

can't control his flame.

But he'll be better after his glass at noon." "My goodness," remarked

Mrs. McBlythe, "he certainly does have a hard time keeping that flame

on his head." "Yes, and it was like that almost every day before we

diagnosed his DFS. Tony was always so busy chasing his own flame

that he couldn't join in what the rest of us were doing.

Since he started drinking quiescence, he's been like a

new boy — a much happier boy."

Just then, two girls approached the mothers. One was crying and

holding her arm. "Bradley is being mean to us," she complained.

"Yeah, and he burned me on my arm," sobbed her companion.

Mrs. McBlythe scanned the playground for the Payne boy, another of

Randall's classmates. When she caught sight of him, he was using his

flame like a blowtorch to scatter a group of children and disrupt their

game. He laughed wickedly, but fell silent as the mothers drew near.

"I didn't do anything!" he protested. "It was an accident!" "Tell that to

the principal," said Mrs. McBlythe as she marched him into the school.

That evening, Mrs. McBlythe attended another meeting of the DFS support group. Mrs. Payne chaired the meeting, and she seemed quite upset as she made her opening comments. "Today an incident occurred at school which is becoming far too common for our DFS children. My own son was unfairly reprimanded by the principal for allegedly 'attacking' other children with his flame." After stopping to glare at Mrs. McBlythe, she went on.

"And this is not the first time this has happened. Everyone in this room knows that our children cannot control their flames. They should not be punished for their disability!"

She paused to acknowledge the applause, and then continued. "Our speaker tonight is Mr. Gudgeon, an attorney who specializes in the rights of handicapped children. He has been quite successful in convincing schools to take the steps necessary to provide an appropriate education for the DFS child." And with that she stepped aside, throwing one last angry look in Mrs. McBlythe's direction. "I can see where Bradley gets his disposition," thought Mrs. McBlythe. Mr. Gudgeon delivered a lengthy speech about various parties' rights and responsibilities. Afterwards he assured everyone he was available for free consultations.

After the meeting, Mrs. McBlythe was surprised to see Mrs. Payne waiting for her in the parking lot. "I can't believe you had the nerve to show up tonight after what you did to my son today." Mrs. McBlythe felt the blood rush to her cheeks as she replied, "I was just doing my job as playground monitor. If one child deliberately injures another, it must be reported to the principal." Mrs. Payne's face contorted as her flame crept closer to Mrs. McBlythe. "But you know that Bradley has DFS — just like your son. It's not his fault." Then she stomped off, screaming back over her shoulder, "HE CAN'T CONTROL HIMSELF!"

When she arrived home that night, Mrs. McBlythe was disappointed Randall was not waiting for her with a new trick or design. She mentioned this to her husband, who reminded her that ever since he began drinking quiescence, Randall no longer seemed interested in entertaining himself or others with his unique flame. The more they thought about it, the more they realized that what was once Randall's most extraordinary feature was now simply... ordinary.

Several days later, the principal asked Mrs. McBlythe to help in the office during lunch while the school secretary was out of the building. Shortly after arriving, Mrs. McBlythe was surprised to see the school nurse wheel a large machine into the office. She inquired about its purpose, and the nurse explained that since so many students were now drinking quiescence, the most efficient method of distribution was this dispensing machine. "Plus," she added, "the little ones seem to really enjoy the colorful lights."

Mrs. McBlythe then watched with great surprise as a line of young children formed in front of the dispenser. One by one they dutifully approached the machine, held out their cups, and drank what the machine dispensed. As they walked away, the flames on top of each head burned with a consistent, uniform glow. When Tony Turbeaux reached to fill his cup, his flame appeared ready to leap from his head. After he drank, the flame stayed right where it was supposed to be. "Hi Mom," said Randall as he took his turn. Bradley Payne drained his own cup then shoved Randall, knocking him to the ground. "Excuse me," he sneered, sticking his tongue out at Mrs. McBlythe.

As children continued to file into the office, Mrs. McBlythe began to wonder if there were any students who did <u>not</u> drink quiescence. Had Defective Flicker Syndrome reached epidemic proportions in Flintville? Or was something else happening? Perhaps some children — like Tony — really cannot control their flames. And for some — like Bradley — their supposed 'disability' conceals other problems. But surely some children's flames are simply... different. If only one type of flame is acceptable, these children automatically become defective. Clearly uniformity could be produced, but at what cost?

54

That night, while Randall lay sleeping,

his mother poured the bottle of

quiescence down the sink.

From that day forward, Randall's flame once again burned in the brightest and most extraordinary manner. His tricks grew more imaginative and his designs more intricate.

Mrs. Steadfast believed the McBlythes were making a serious mistake, and she predicted dire consequences for Randall as he advanced into upper grade levels. Dr. Vaticinate shrugged her shoulders and muttered something about 'denial.'

But Randall's parents were glad to have their entertaining and unpredictable son back again. They came to understand that to some eyes — and in some situations — Randall burned too brightly. But to them, he burned just right.

About the Author

Dr. David J. Welsh is a psychologist with a private practice in Fort Worth, Texas. For the past fifteen years he has worked extensively with school-age children in a variety of contexts. During that time he has grown increasingly alarmed at the large numbers of children diagnosed and labelled with a variety of supposed disorders requiring special treatments and modifications. In an attempt to draw attention to this phenomenon and raise questions about its underlying rationale and long-term implications, he created the story of *The Boy Who Burned Too Brightly.*

A popular speaker and trainer who regularly appears before audiences across the country, Dr. Welsh can be contacted at Jones, Welsh & Associates, 6040 Camp Bowie, Fort Worth, TX 76116, (817) 735-8299.

About the Illustrator

A recent graduate of Amherst College, Brandon Bolt currently is pursuing a professional career as a cartoonist and illustrator. *The Boy Who Burned Too Brightly* is his first large-scale work.